This igloo book belongs to:

....

Contents

igloobooks

Published in 2017
by Igloo Books Ltd, Cottage Farm, Sywell, NN6 0BJ
www.igloobooks.com

Written by Xanna Chown
Illustrated by Dean Gray

Cover designed by Lee Italiano & Justine Ablett
Interiors designed by Justine Ablett
Edited by Stephanie Moss

STA002 0617
2 4 6 8 10 9 7 5 3 1
ISBN 978-1-78670-358-3

Printed and manufactured in China

5 Minute Tales

Bedtime Stories

igloobooks

Animal Explorers

Late one afternoon, Pete was daydreaming about exploring in deepest Africa, when Mum appeared.

This is Jess. She's just moved in next door. Now you two can play together,

she said.

Oh, no. She'll only want to play **boring** games,

thought Pete.

4

Pete frowned and sat in silence, so Jess stared out of the window.

Let's go exploring in the garden,

said Jess.

There's nothing interesting out there except silly bugs,

complained Pete.

5

Jess ignored Pete and grabbed his safari hat and binoculars, then she found his torch. When they got outside, she made a den, hidden in the bushes.

It's so the wild animals can't see us, she said.

There **aren't** any wild animals, scoffed Pete.

Suddenly, there was a funny grunting noise and a **strange** shadow appeared on the lawn, right before their eyes.

Pete couldn't believe it. He **scrambled** after Jess, as she leaped out of the den and chased after the elephant, but it had gone.
Then, she pointed to a line of paw prints that led near the bushes.

There, it's a **tiger**,

she said, just as a shadow **stalked** along the wall.

Run!

cried Pete.

He and Jess **dashed** across the lawn and hid from the tiger behind the garden shed. Next, Pete pointed to a long-necked shadow, **swaying** by the washing line.

Look! There's a **giraffe** in our garden,

he said.

Back to the den,

whispered Jess.

Suddenly, another shadow **loomed** over them, blocking their escape.

It's a **gorilla!**

said Jess.

It's a **bear!**

said Pete.

The shadow got **closer** and **closer**, until...

They **scrambled** across the lawn and **dived** back into their den.

Pete shone his torch and saw that it wasn't a gorilla, or a bear, at all.
It was Dad, carrying a tray with some sandwiches and drinks on it.

Then, Pete and Jess peeped out of their den and saw Buddy playing with a sock from the washing basket. His shadow looked like an elephant!

Pickles' shadow looked like a tiger...

... and Mum's shadow looked like a giraffe.

Pete and Jess laughed. They sat down to munch on their treats and as they chatted about their exploring adventure, they both smiled.

I'm glad you came round to play,

said Pete.

Me too. Thanks for joining in with the game,

said Jess.

Pete felt really happy. He was pleased Jess was going to be his new friend and she was definitely anything but boring!

Moon Magic

Billy didn't like bedtime. He was scared of the dark. Mum tucked him in and told him not to worry, but then there was a soft **TAP-TAP** at the window.

There's a **monster** outside!

squeaked Billy.

There's no such thing as monsters, said Mum, smiling...

... but Billy didn't believe her.

Come on, I'll show you how beautiful it can be outside at night, said Mum.

So, Billy took a deep breath and followed Mum into the garden.

It was dark outside and Billy could hardly see anything in the
shadowy garden. He gripped Mum's hand, tightly.

We need a bit of
moon magic,

whispered Mum.

Moon, moon,
big and **bright**,
show us the beauty
of the night,

she said.

As Mum spoke, the moon came out from behind the clouds and flooded the garden with light.

The beautiful beams **danced** on the garden pond. Billy gasped, as they glittered and sparkled.

Even the stars in the sky seemed extra twinkly.

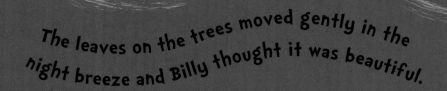

The leaves on the trees moved gently in the night breeze and Billy thought it was beautiful.

Oh, it was just a tree tapping at my window. It wasn't a monster at all!

said Billy.

Mum laughed, as Billy watched the long branches **swaying** to and fro.

See, Billy. It was nothing to be afraid of after all,

she said, with a kind smile.

In the moonlight, they saw a baby bunny **hop** across the lawn and disappear into a sandy burrow...

... then, some tiny birds **fluttered** up to their nest.

Look, they're all going to bed,

said Mum.

Seeing the sleepy animals made Billy yawn.

Soon, Billy was snuggled up in his cosy bed again.

Can you leave the curtains open tonight, Mum?

he asked, sleepily.

In no time at all, Billy was fast asleep with the moonbeams shining on his face.

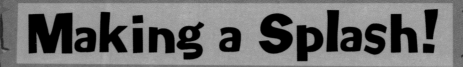

Making a Splash!

I can't believe my birthday party is at Pirate Play Pool!

cried Jack, excitedly. He loved swimming.

Where else would a little pirate go?

joked Dad.

22

Jack's best friends, Tom and Alfie, were waiting in the changing room. They gave Jack a special swashbuckling swimsuit as a present.

I feel just like a pirate! I hope I'm tall enough for the Turbo Tentacle slide,

said Jack.

He went to the octopus height chart and **cheered** happily when he saw that he was.

Jack began to climb the slide steps. He went **higher** and **higher**. From the top, the pool below looked tiny and far away. All of a sudden, Jack's tummy felt funny and he started to get dizzy.

Alfie and Tom **zoomed** down the slide, but Jack started to cry.

Don't worry,

said a friendly attendant. He helped Jack back down the steps.

Jack sat by the baby pool, watching the younger children SPLISH-SPLASH in the water.

This is where I belong,

he thought, sadly.

25

Then, Jack's friends came to give him a hug.

Come on, Jack, pirates don't belong in the baby pool, said Tom.

But a **real** pirate wouldn't be scared to go down the water slide, sniffed Jack.

He might be at first, but he'd do it anyway, said Alfie, smiling.

Then, Tom gave Jack his special wristband that had a cool skull-and-crossbones pattern on it.

> Why don't you try wearing this? It's from Captain Bravebeard's **magical** treasure chest. It will make you feel fearless!

he said.

To his surprise, Jack did feel much more brave with the wristband. The slide still looked super-scary, but he wanted to try again.

The three friends climbed the steps together. Jack's heart **fluttered** and his legs **wobbled** in fear as he reached the top. Then, he looked at his magic band.

Pirates are brave,

he thought.

Jack took a deep breath and...

... whoosh!

He **whizzed** down the slide, feeling scared and excited, all at once.

Splash!

Jack was in the pool.

Splish! Splosh!

Alfie and Tom whooshed in right behind him.

This is **amazing!** I don't feel scared at all,

cried Jack, sliding down one more time.

Now you're a real pirate!

cheered Tom.

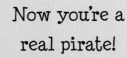

29

The Magic Teddy

Annie was excited about staying at Gran's house, until she realised her teddy wasn't in her overnight bag.

I won't be able to sleep without him,

she whimpered, beginning to cry.

Don't worry, I have just the thing,

said Gran.

Gran fetched a tatty-looking teddy. He was lovely and soft, but he wasn't Annie's special teddy. Annie still felt upset.

I won't be able to sleep,

she said again, closing her eyes.

Teddy might surprise you,

said Gran, smiling and kissing Annie goodnight.

Just then, something soft
tickled Annie's nose.
She opened her eyes to see
Gran's teddy surrounded by
twinkly sparkles.

He had come to life!

Annie touched his paw and
suddenly, she was in a
magical fairground made
of soft, cosy pillows.

Everywhere Annie looked, more **magical** teddies were enjoying the rides. There were swings, slides and much more.

Annie **squealed** in delight, as she watched the teddies whizz down a helter-skelter.

WHOOSH!

Annie giggled, as she held Teddy's hand tight, and **boinged** up
and down on a super-springy bouncy-castle mattress.

She **jumped...**

... bumped...

... and bounced...

... higher than the fluffy-pillow walls.
It was so much fun!

Annie and Teddy **whizzed** down a water slide that **splashed** into a bubble-bath river.

They **zoomed** around in a dodgem car that looked like a slipper.

They even won a **magical** alarm clock at the **funniest** coconut shy Annie had ever seen!

Just then, Annie began to feel very sleepy. She gave a big yawn and before she knew it, Annie was flying through the air with Teddy.

With a twinkle and a sparkle, she was back in bed at Gran's again. Annie felt so sleepy, she snuggled up with Teddy.

I must tell Gran that her teddy is magical,

she said and fell fast asleep.

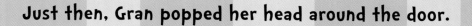
Just then, Gran popped her head around the door.

I know he is, Annie.
He always has been!
Goodnight, both of you.
Sleep tight,

said Gran, softly.

37

The Sleepover

It was Elsa's first sleepover with her best friends, Bella and Ivy. They had already changed into their cosiest PJs, when they went downstairs to get some tasty snacks from the kitchen.

Remember to shut the fridge door. We don't want the new puppy, Benji, taking any food!

called Mum.

Okay, Mum,

said Elsa, but she was too busy choosing delicious treats to listen.

The three girls ran upstairs excitedly, giggling and dropping cheesy puffs on the carpet as they went.

We're going to have so much fun,

said Elsa.

The friends snuggled in their PJs and chatted. They ate their snacks and, just as Elsa was about to tell a spooky ghost story, the clock struck twelve. Suddenly, there was a strange noise from downstairs.

Something is **snuffling** around,

said Bella.

But... what is it?

asked Ivy.

I don't know, but I think we should find out. Follow me,

said Elsa.

She grabbed a torch and they set off to investigate.

The girls crept down the stairs and followed the sound into the kitchen. Elsa **SCREAMED** and dropped the torch on Ivy's foot.

Ow! cried Ivy, **jumping** up and down. She bumped into Bella and spilt Benji's water.

Shh! What's that noise?

asked Elsa.

Ivy turned to see something disappearing down the hallway.

It's a **snake!**

she cried.

The girls raced out of the kitchen, just in time to see a **mysterious** creature slip through the lounge door.

It's vanished,

gasped Ivy.

They followed it into the dark room, but Elsa saw something was behind one of the curtains.

Suddenly, a dark shape **bounded** out from behind the curtain, **bumping** into a table. It knocked over a tall vase of flowers that fell onto the floor with a

CRASH!

The girls all **screamed** and looked at each other in fright.

Quickly, Elsa grabbed a blanket and threw it over the shape. The girls breathed a sigh of relief as it **skidded** to a halt. Then it disappeared behind the sofa, with the blanket draped over its head, like a ghost.

Then, the girls jumped in fright as a **slurping**, **chewing** sound filled the room.

Nobody knew, but nobody wanted to peep behind the sofa, either!

CLICK! Someone switched on the light. It was Elsa's mum.

What's all this noise?

she asked. Just then, Benji slunk out from behind the sofa with a string of sausages.

It's Benji! What a naughty monster,

cried Elsa.

47

Benji wouldn't have got the sausages if you hadn't left the fridge door open,

said Mum.

Sorry, Mum. I promise to listen to you next time,

said Elsa.

The girls had a nice hot drink and went to bed, after closing the fridge door, of course!

48